Who Loves Mr Tubs?

D0336259

For Bebe Waddell
B.M.

For Tamlyn
S.H.

EGMONT

We bring stories to life

Book Band: Purple

First published in Great Britain 2006
This Reading Ladder edition published 2016
by Egmont UK Limited
The Yellow Building, 1 Nicholas Road, London W11 4AN
Text copyright © Bel Mooney 2006
Illustrations copyright © Susan Hellard 2006
The author and illustrator have asserted their moral rights
ISBN 978 1 4052 8205 5
www.egmont.co.uk
A CIP catalogue record for this title is available from the British Library.
Printed in Singapore
43937/5

All rights reserved. No part of this publication may be reproduced,
stored in a retrieval system, or transmitted, in any form or by any means,
electronic, mechanical, photocopying, recording or otherwise, without the
prior permission of the publisher and copyright owner.
Stay safe online. Egmont is not responsible for content hosted by third parties.

Series consultant: Nikki Gamble

MIX
Paper
FSC FSC® C018306

Bel Mooney ♥ Susan Hellard

Who Loves Mr Tubs?

Reading Ladder

Mr Tubs was always pleased on Kitty's birthday, because she was so happy. He liked to see her smile.

Kitty put Mr Tubs down to open her presents. When she came to the parcel from her aunt and uncle and cousin Melissa she had a surprise.

Mr Tubs watched Kitty take her new doll out of the box and hold her up in the air.

Just then Kitty's friends Rosie and
Anita arrived for tea. They loved
Kitty's new toy and both admired her
trendy clothes.

Later, they put Kitty's new CD on and danced around the room. Mum joined in, saying she loved the song.

9

At last it was time for Kitty to go to bed. Suddenly she spotted Mr Tubs on the floor and picked him up. She gave him a big hug and whispered that Suki would be his new best friend.

Kitty settled down in bed to read one
of her new books, with Suki on one side
and Mr Tubs on the other.

She said thank you to Mum for a
lovely birthday.

In the middle of the night Mr Tubs

dreamed that he was climbing a tree.

He wanted to find the honeycomb that

the bees had left in the branches.

But just when he got near the honey a

beautiful, bad bird flew at his head.

She sang loudly in his ear,

telling him to

go away.

Go away!

Mmmm –
yummy honey.

Zzzzstop
zzzzstealing,
Mr Tubzzzzzz!

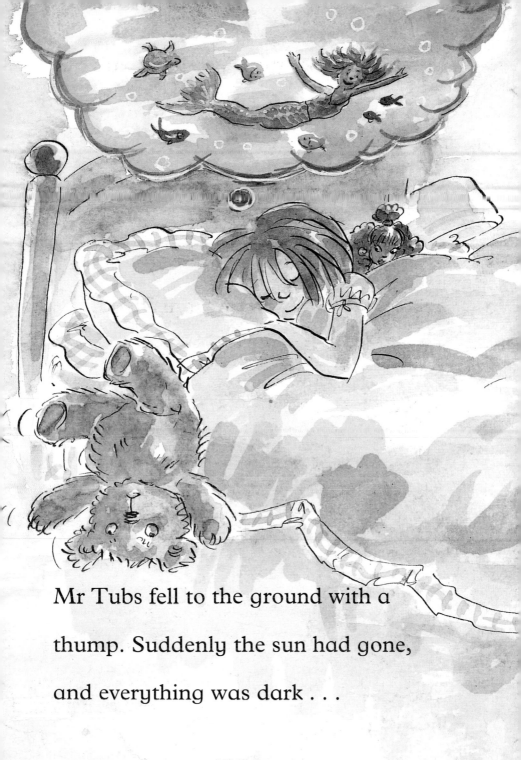

Mr Tubs fell to the ground with a
thump. Suddenly the sun had gone,
and everything was dark . . .

In the morning Kitty was late for
school as usual. Rushing around, she
didn't notice Mr Tubs on the floor.

Later, Mum came in to make the bed and found Mr Tubs. She put him on the chair with Suki by his side.

The next week, Mr Tubs couldn't

believe it. He sat on the chair . . . and

sat . . . and sat . . . while Kitty took

Suki everywhere.

They went to

Rosie's house, and

Rosie's big sister loved the cool doll.

They went shopping for clothes with

Kitty's mum.

They went to the library to

look for a book on dinosaurs.

They met Anita at the ice cream shop.

They watched TV downstairs with

Dan.

All the time Mr Tubs waited,

trying to be brave, feeling

very lonely in Kitty's room.

I don't really mind being on my own.

He could almost feel dust falling

on him, as he waited for Kitty

to take him out again,

like she used to.

Each night Kitty put Suki on the chair next to Mr Tubs, and told them to look after each other. She'd decided that she was old enough to sleep all by herself.

Each night three different dreams
bobbed about the little bedroom.

One afternoon Baby Tom
just cried and cried.
Mum tried the dummy,
but it didn't work.

She tried the
musical mobile
but it didn't work.

She tried singing a song but Tom just
cried all the more. At last she had to
walk out of the room because she felt
cross and upset and worried –
all at the same time.

She was standing by the door of

Kitty's room when she spotted

Mr Tubs, still waiting on the chair.

Quickly she picked him up and popped

him into Tom's cot.

Now, Tom, look who's come to see you!

Waaaa- waaaa- waaaa!

Hurray! Somebody wants me!

It really was very noisy in that cot.

Aaaaah-
aaaaah-
aaaaaah!

I've got to do
something
about this.

Tom yelled and yelled right next to

Mr Tubs's ears. And the baby's tears

started to make his old fur all wet.

Nobody really knows how bears can talk to babies. But they can. Mr Tubs started up his most smooth, purring growl, deep inside, and he wished Baby Tom a peaceful sleep with every little bit of his old furry heart.

Later, when Mum tiptoed into his room to check, Tom was fast asleep, with one arm round the old bear. She was very happy.

When Kitty came home from school
she went up to her room to fetch Suki.
Right away she noticed Mr Tubs
wasn't in his usual place.

Kitty ran all over the house looking for Mr Tubs. Suddenly she felt guilty because she knew she hadn't played with him, and she wanted to put things right.

Mum took her into the baby's room.

Tom was still fast asleep, cuddling

Mr Tubs. Kitty stared into the cot.

Mum said that since she was too

grown-up for her bear, she should

give him to Tom.

I don't want to.
It's not fair.

It is fair!
You always play
with Suki now.

Hello, Kitty.

Kitty pretended she didn't mind. She
went into her bedroom and picked
up Suki.

Come on,
Suki, we'll go
and watch TV.

The room
seemed empty
without Mr Tubs,
but Kitty decided
not to think about it.

But later, when Kitty tried to make a den with the sofa cushions like she used to, Suki didn't look as if she enjoyed it. Kitty remembered it was one of Mr Tubs's favourite games.

Mr Tubs was quite happy in Tom's cot. It was warm and cosy, and he felt loved. When Mum took the baby downstairs he went too, because Tom loved to hug him – even though he was nearly the same size as him. Mr Tubs felt part of the family again.

Tom loves that teddy!

And at bedtime he liked the songs Mum sang to the baby. Inside his head he joined in. That made him sleepy too.

'Go to sleep now, goodnight, In your bed soft and white,

All the creatures of the day, Must have rest from work and play.'

Mmmmf . . . mmmmf . . . snore.

31

A few days later Kitty felt ill. She
sniffed and snuffled and sneezed so
much Mum said she should go to bed.
Her nose was red and she felt very
sorry for herself. Dad said she would
soon feel better.

Upstairs now, Kitty.

At-tish-ooooh!

Kitty went upstairs and put her
pyjamas on.

She looked at her bed and knew she

wanted someone
to cuddle.

I want
Mr Tubs.

No – I'm your
favourite,
Kitty!

She looked at Suki and knew she
wouldn't do. Suki was cool, but
not cuddly.

Kitty crept into Tom's room. He was fast asleep. Mr Tubs lay there, looking up at her. Very carefully she picked him up and <u>held</u> him tight. But just then Tom woke up and started to cry.

Shhhhh.

Mum and Dad came rushing upstairs.
They told Kitty she should leave
Mr Tubs with Tom because the
baby loved him now.
Kitty was very cross.

Kitty rushed into her room, grabbed Suki, and jumped into bed. But her lovely new doll felt hard and cold, and Kitty suddenly knew the truth. She liked Suki but she didn't love her.

So am I, Kitty.

I'm sorry, Suki.

Loving a toy was something that happened over a very long time.

When Mum and Dad came in to see her, Kitty tried not to cry. Dad knew what was wrong, and so did Mum. They had to come up with a plan to put it right. But they all knew Tom would be unhappy without the old bear.

Then Kitty had her brilliant idea.
Mr Tubs was a bear, but he wasn't the
only bear in the world. Even if he was
the best bear. Mr Tubs belonged with
her. But if she took him back, she must
give Tom something in return. The
thought made her feel much better.

A couple of days later Kitty was well again. She emptied her money box and put the money in a little pile. Dad said he would take her shopping. She went to say goodbye to Mr Tubs, who was sitting with Tom on Mum's knee.

While they were out Mr Tubs played

with Tom on the floor. They played

'Pull Teddy Along By The Ear' and

'Hold Teddy

Upside Down

By His Feet'

and 'Pinch

Teddy's Nose'.

Hurry up, Kitty.

Mr Tubs thought it was all great fun.

But it did make him rather tired.

At last Kitty ran into the room, waving

a bag from the toy shop. She pulled out

a brand-new bear for Tom. He was

smaller than Mr Tubs, and a darker

brown with light brown paws.

Look what we've got for Tom!

Oh, what a sweet little bear!

Mr Tubs thought the bear looked very

nice. Tom smiled and waved his hands.

Mum told Kitty she must be careful and not take Mr Tubs back too soon. So all afternoon she played with Tom and Mr Tubs. She asked Tom what they should call the new bear. He gurgled 'Buh-buh-buh,' and she clapped her hands. 'Yes!' she cried. 'We'll call him Bubba Bear.'

Kitty put the two bears on the sofa and went to have her tea. She told Mr Tubs he had to look after Bubba and tell him what to do. Mr Tubs agreed.

You help him, Mr Tubs.

All right, Kitty.

He knew that Bubba might not understand that being a child's bear is really a very important job. He was a rather young bear after all.

Mr Tubs told Bubba all the jobs he had to do to look after Baby Tom. He made sure he knew the List of Very Important Duties of a Teddy.

He had to put up with getting dirty.

He had to drive away bad dreams with long, low growls.

He had to make sure Tom didn't ever feel lonely.

He had to be Tom's best friend and

play with him always.

He had to be loyal to Tom and love

him for ever.

Can you remember all that, Bubba?

Bubba listened and said

he would do his best.

Oh, I'll try really hard, Mr Tubs.

When it was Tom's bedtime Kitty put both bears in the cot, but put Tom's arms around Bubba. The little bear looked very happy, and so did Tom. Mr Tubs sang his special soft growly song to help them both get to sleep. Then, very quietly, Kitty took him out of the cot.

Time for you to come home to my room, Mr Tubs.

At last! But what about Suki?

Kitty made a space on the shelf where she kept her favourite books. She picked Suki up and stroked her lovely dark hair. 'You know I really, really like you, Suki,' she said, 'but you're such a special doll I'm going to put you up where I can admire you. Then when Rosie and Anita come to play we'll get you down.'

Everybody can see you up here.

That's my clever Kitty.

Mr Tubs lay on Kitty's pillow. She sat on the bed and looked at him. 'Can you forgive me?' she whispered. 'I was so excited about my new doll that I forgot about you. But then I realised how much I missed cuddling you. I'm soooo sorry, Mr Tubs.'

You know who loves you, Mr Tubs – don't you?

You do, Kitty.

The look in Mr Tubs's black eyes told her it didn't matter. As long as they were back together again – for ever.